Colonel Purple Turtle's Purple Turtle Journal

Written by **RocknoceroS**

Pictures by Missy Sheldrake

*Thanks to our families, fans,
and friends for their continued support!*

Colonel Purple Turtle's Purple Turtle Journal
Ashway Press

First Edition 2011
Text Copyright © 2011 by Rocknoceros
Illustrations Copyright © 2011 by Melissa Sheldrake
Acrylic on canvas

ISBN 978-0-9754575-1-1

Printed and manufactured by Friesens Corporation in Altona, MB, Canada
July, 2011
Job #66660

For more information:
ASHWAY PRESS
5624 DOUBLETREE CIRCLE BIRMINGHAM AL 35242

To order more books: www.givingmeaway.com

www.rocknoceros.com
www.muralsbymissy.com

Art Director: Kendra Peine
Design & Layout: Becky Bryant
www.beckybryantdesign.com

I am **COLONEL PURPLE TURTLE** and I live in Soggy Bog.
Lots of other animals live here, and some come to visit me from faraway places.
I like to write in my journal about all of my interesting friends.

HARRY ELEFANTE

is a pachyderm who comes
to visit each year.

He is a good *dancer* and loves
to play hopscotch and baseball.

He uses his trunk to
pick flowers, lift heavy
things, and water
our gardens.

The **FROGS** are amphibians who like the rain and fog.

They live in hollow logs where they bake fly pies and eat french flies.

A **SCHOLARLY OWL** lives atop

the old oak tree by the pond.

He always has LOTS to say.

His riddles are *mysteries*, his mysteries

are clues, and he spends most of his time

feathers-deep in research.

I know he is very smart,

but I rarely understand

what he is saying.

Still pondering the owl's words,

I saw something quite *beautiful*.

Not far from the owl's home,

a **BUTTERFLY** had just

sprouted her wings.

She was taking flying

lessons from **MR. MEADOWLARK**.

My tiniest friends in Soggy Bog are

the **LADYBIRD BEETLES**.

I try to bring them a box of aphids

to munch whenever I drop by.

Did you know that they are

also called lady bugs,

and some are orange?

When the weather gets rough in Soggy Bog, friends and neighbors work together to help each other stay safe.

PIRATE HARVEY and first mate TRUFFLES have anchored their schooner outside Soggy Bog.

I could hear the crew of pirate cats celebrating another successful voyage as I waited to welcome them ashore.

My friend **ROCKY THE DOG**

owns a very tidy hardware store.

He sells rakes and mulch and hammers

and the best wax for my turtle shell.

Rocky's a great friend who

is always *quick* to share

a soda pop.

TRUMAN COYOTE lives in a cozy den

next to Rocky's Hardware store.

He is a writer like ME,

though he uses a **typewriter**

while I use a *feather quill.*

Many animals live in *Soggy Bog*, while others visit from all over the world. You've met a few of them, but what is your favorite animal?

ABOUT RocknoceroS

Rocknoceros is a band from Fairfax, Virginia that makes original music for children of all ages. *Colonel Purple Turtle's Purple Turtle Journal* is their debut book, and the text and illustrations in the book were inspired by the songs found on their CD, *Colonel Purple Turtle*. The band consists of Coach Cotton, Williebob, and Boogie Woogie Bennie, and performs up and down the East Coast in theaters, libraries, parks and schools for thousands of families annually. Visit **www.rocknoceros.com** to learn more.

ABOUT MISSY SHELDRAKE

Missy Sheldrake is a freelance artist residing in Northern Virginia. Surrounded by the loving support of her family, she spends her days either playing with her young son or painting murals for local businesses and residents. Missy's whimsical style reflects her love of nature and her belief that anything can become something magical with just a touch of imagination. You can see more of her artwork by visiting her website: **www.muralsbymissy.com**.